MY GRANDPA IS A DINOSAUR

RICHARD FAIRGRAY AND TERRY JONES

COLOURING BY TARA BLACK

For Paul Eiding,
a grandpa who will one
day be a dinosaur.

PUFFIN

First published in New Zealand by Penguin Random House New Zealand, 2016

1 3 5 7 9 10 8 6 4 2

Text © Richard Fairgray and Terry Jones, 2016
Illustrations © Richard Fairgray, 2016

Design by Kate Barraclough © Penguin Random House New Zealand
Illustration colouring by Tara Black
Printed and bound in China by Leo Paper Products Ltd

A catalogue record for this book is available from the National Library of New Zealand.
ISBN 978-0-14-350719-2

penguinrandomhouse.co.nz

Wanda knew there was something weird about her family,
and it wasn't her older sister.

It wasn't her bratty brother.

It wasn't even her mum or dad.

The thing that was so weird about Wanda's family . . .

. . . was that her grandpa was a dinosaur.

All his pants had to have tail holes.

At the Grandparents' Day Picnic he was
the only one who ate an entire tree.

Palaeontologists were always following his footprints.

Mum even fitted the car with a special seat for him.

When he jumped in the pool he splashed out all the water.

And every Hallowe'en he dressed as the ghost of a dinosaur.

But the weirdest part of all was that no one would believe Wanda when she told them.

She tried to tell her sister.

But her sister didn't believe her.

She tried to tell her friend.

But her friend didn't believe her either.

She tried to tell her mum.

But even her mum didn't believe her.

So Wanda decided to ask him herself.

"Yes," smiled Grandpa. "Of course I am."

For the rest of that day Wanda and her grandpa
had more fun together than ever before.

And that evening, when her grandpa took her back
to his retirement home, Wanda realised . . .

. . . that her grandpa wasn't the only dinosaur after all.

Not even close.